Prehistoric Creatures

Dinosaur Tails and Armor

Joanne Mattern

Reading consultant: Susan Nations, M.Ed., author/literacy coach/consultant

WR WEEKLY READER
EARLY LEARNING LIBRARY

Please visit our web site at: **www.earlyliteracy.cc**
For a free color catalog describing Weekly Reader® Early Learning Library's
list of high-quality books, call 1-877-445-5824 (USA) or 1-800-387-3178 (Canada).
Weekly Reader® Early Learning Library's fax: (414) 336-0164.

Library of Congress Cataloging-in-Publication Data

Mattern, Joanne, 1963-
    Dinosaur tails and armor / Joanne Mattern.
      p. cm. — (Prehistoric creatures)
    Includes bibliographical references and index.
    ISBN 0-8368-4899-3 (lib. bdg.)
    ISBN 0-8368-4906-X (softcover)
    1. Dinosaur—Juvenile literature. I. Title. II. Series.
QE861.5.M348   2005
567.9—dc22   2005042870

This edition first published in 2006 by
Weekly Reader® Early Learning Library
A Member of the WRC Media Family of Companies
330 West Olive Street, Suite 100
Milwaukee, WI 53212 USA

Managing editor: Valerie J. Weber
Art direction and design: Tammy West

Illustrations: John Alston, Lisa Alderson, Dougal Dixon, Simon Mendez, Luis Rey

Printed in the United States of America

1 2 3 4 5 6 7 8 9 09 08 07 06 05

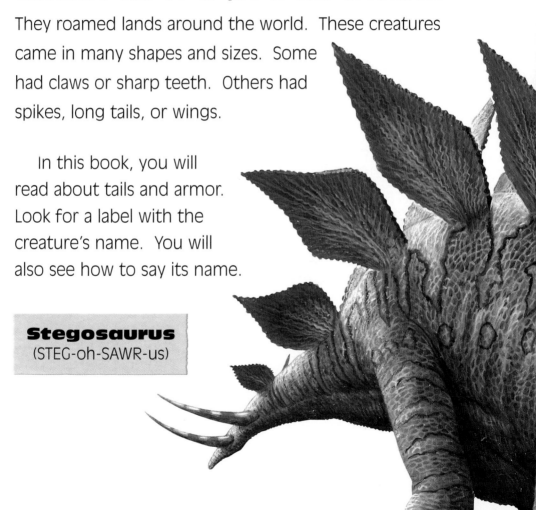

Long before there were people there were dinosaurs and other prehistoric creatures.

They roamed lands around the world. These creatures came in many shapes and sizes. Some had claws or sharp teeth. Others had spikes, long tails, or wings.

In this book, you will read about tails and armor. Look for a label with the creature's name. You will also see how to say its name.

Stegosaurus
(STEG-oh-SAWR-us)

Long Tails

What good are tails? Tails can help an animal keep its balance. An animal can also use its tail to hit other creatures. Some animals use their tails to help them steer in water or air.

Look at the long tails on these dinosaurs! Some of these dinosaurs were small. Some were big. All of them had tails that were much longer than the rest of their bodies.

Prosauropods
(proh-sawr-OP-ods)

Dangerous Tails

Some dinosaurs used their long, thin tails like whips. They could swing their tails around and hit **predators**, or animals that hunted them.

Other dinosaurs had thick, heavy clubs at the ends of their tails. A club would be a good weapon if it hit another dinosaur!

Sauropods
(SAWR-uh-pods)

5

Ankylosaurid
(AN-kye-loh-SAWR-id)

A Clubbed Tail

This dinosaur also had a big club at the end of its tail. It used its tail like a powerful weapon against other animals.

A thick, heavy skin of **armor** covered its body. Sharp spikes pointed out from this armor. All these features helped the dinosaur protect itself.

Swing That Tail!

Watch out for this dinosaur's tail! When this creature swung its clubbed tail, other dinosaurs got out of the way. The bones in the bottom of its tail were joined together to hold up the heavy club. This dinosaur was so fierce it could even fight off a T. Rex!

Euoplocephalus
(YOU-oh-ploe-SEF-ah-lus)

A Pack of Long Tails

During the 1940s, scientists discovered the fossils of a large group of these dinosaurs. Because they found so many fossils together, scientists thought the animals might travel in packs.

These dinosaurs had long tails. Their tails might have helped these creatures balance when they ran.

Too Long for Land

This dinosaur's tail was two times the length of its body. Its tail was so long that the creature probably could not walk well on land. It swam in the water where its long tail could help push it. The tail helped the animal steer, too.

Hovasaurus
(HOE-vah-SAWR-us)

Paddling Along

This early reptile lived in the water and ate shellfish like crabs and shrimp. Its tail was shaped like a paddle, and webbed feet helped it swim. It could also walk along the ocean floor. It came up to the surface to breathe.

Placodus
(PLAK-uh-dus)

Tails in the Water

Look at the long tails on these sea creatures. These
lizards had long, flat tails. The tails helped them
move through the water.

Mosasaurs could be big or small. Some were
the size of a cat or dog. Others were longer than
a shark!

Flying High

Flying dinosaurs had tails, too. These creatures are called pterosaurs. Their long tails helped them keep their balance in the air. Pterosaurs were the largest creatures to fly through the skies.

Rhamphorhynchoid
(RAM-foe-RING-koyd)

Sordes
(SOR-dees)

Tails for Steering

A flap of skin grew at the end of this flying reptile's long, stiff tail. Scientists think this flap helped the creature steer through the sky. It might also have helped the animal keep its balance while it flew.

Is It a Bird or a Dinosaur?

Is it a bird? Is it a dinosaur? This creature had a short tail and front limbs like a bird. Its fossil also showed there were feathers on its arms and tail. Scientists do not think this creature could fly. Its front limbs were not strong enough to hold its heavy body up in the air.

Protarchaeopteryx
(PROH-tahr-kee-OP-ter-iks)

Icaronycteris
(ick-uh-rah-NIK-ter-us)

Prehistoric Bat

This creature is a prehistoric bat. It looks a lot like the bats that fly around today. It has a longer tail than today's bats. Its wings did not connect to its tail. The wings on today's bats are attached to their tails.

Armored Dinosaurs

Some dinosaurs were covered with armor. This armor protected the dinosaur from predators. Armor could also help in other ways. Scientists think the armor on this dinosaur made its backbone stronger. A strong spine helped the heavy creature carry its weight.

On All Fours

Thick armor covered this dinosaur. The plates of armor looked like leaves standing on its body. The armor protected the creature from predators.

Armor also made the dinosaur very heavy. Its strong legs helped hold up all that weight.

Stegosaurus
(STEG-oh-SAWR-us)

Small but Tough

This dinosaur was only about the size of a cow. Bumpy armor covered its heavy, tough body. Pointy studs stuck out on its back. Small horns pointed out behind its ears, too. That is a lot of protection!

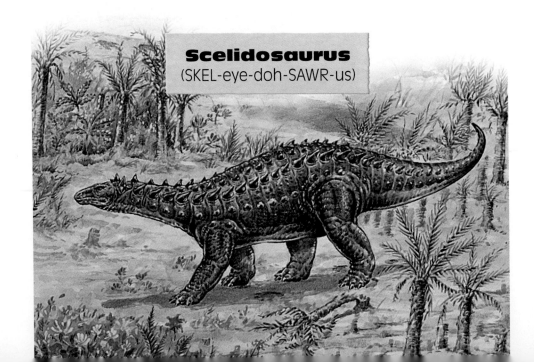

Scelidosaurus
(SKEL-eye-doh-SAWR-us)

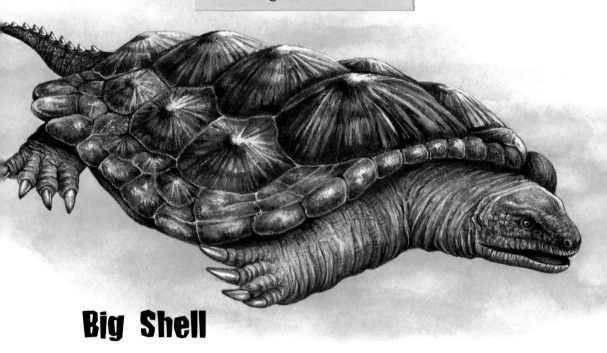

Big Shell

This creature is the oldest known turtle. It moved very slowly, so it could not swim away from predators. The turtle used armor to protect itself. Bones joined together on its back and belly formed its armor.

Placodonts
(PLAK-uh-donts)

Staying Safe

These creatures moved slowly. They could have
been easy prey for predators. To protect
themselves, they had shells on their bodies. Even
though they looked like turtles, they are not related
to today's turtles.

Giant Crocodile

Do you think this creature looks like a crocodile? It was part of the same family. It was also longer than a school bus! It was so huge that it could eat big dinosaurs. This prehistoric reptile had scales and a long tail. Tails and armor helped protect prehistoric creatures.

Deinosuchus
(die-no-SUE-kus)

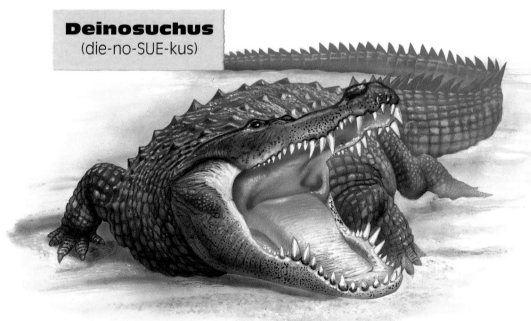

Glossary

armor — protective scales or spikes that cover some animals

balance — the ability to keep steady

fierce — dangerous

fossils — remains of an animal or plant that lived millions of years ago

predators — animals that hunt other animals for food

prehistoric — living in times before written history

pterosaurs — a group of prehistoric creatures that could fly

prey — an animal that is hunted for food

reptile — cold-blooded animal with skin covered in scales or bony plates like armor

scales — small pieces of hard skin

shellfish — sea creatures that have shells

spine — the backbone of an animal

weapon — something that can be used in a fight

For More Information

Books

Ankylosaurus. Rupert Matthews (Heinemann Library)

Bony Back: The Adventure of Stegosaurus. Michael Dahl (Picture Window Books)

Stiff Armor: The Adventure of Ankylosaurus. Michael Dahl (Picture Window Books)

Web Sites

All About Dinosaurs: Ankylosaurus
www.enchantedlearning.com/subjects/dinosaurs/ dinos/Ankylosaurus.shtml
Find a diagram, facts, and a picture of this dinosaur to print out and color on this web site.

Walking with Dinosaurs: Coelophysis
www.abc.net.au/dinosaurs/fact_files/dried/coelophysis.htm
Learn more about Coelophysis and see photos and a video made by computer.

Index

armor 3, 6, 16, 17, 18, 19, 21

balancing 4, 8, 13

bats 15

birds 14

bones 19

breathing 10

clubs 5, 6, 7

crocodile 21

feathers 14

feet 10

flying 12, 13, 14, 15

fossils 8, 14

lizards 11

plates 17

predators 5, 6, 17, 19, 20

prey 20

pterosaurs 12, 13

reptiles 9, 13, 21

scales 21

shellfish 10

shells 19, 20

spikes 6

spine 16

steering 4, 9, 13

Stegosaurus 17

swimming 9, 10, 11, 19

T. Rex 7

turtles 19, 20

weapons 5, 6

wings 15

About the Author

Joanne Mattern is the author of more than 130 books for children. Her favorite subjects are animals, history, sports, and biographies. Joanne lives in New York State with her husband, three young daughters, and three crazy cats.